JACK LONDON

# White Fang

Retold by Rachel Bladon

## MACMILLAN READERS

### ELEMENTARY LEVEL

*Founding Editor:* John Milne

The Macmillan Readers provide a choice of enjoyable reading materials for learners of English. The series is published at six levels – Starter, Beginner, Elementary, Pre-intermediate, Intermediate and Upper.

## Level Control

Information, structure and vocabulary are controlled to suit the students' ability at each level.

## The number of words at each level:

| | |
|---|---|
| Starter | about 300 basic words |
| Beginner | about 600 basic words |
| Elementary | about 1100 basic words |
| Pre-intermediate | about 1400 basic words |
| Intermediate | about 1600 basic words |
| Upper | about 2200 basic words |

## Vocabulary

Some difficult words and phrases in this book are important for understanding the story. Some of these words are explained in the story, some are shown in the pictures, and others are marked with a number like this: ...³. Words with a number are explained in the Glossary at the end of the book.

## Answer Keys

Answer Keys for the *Points for Understanding* and *Exercises* sections can be found at www.macmillanenglish.com/readers

# Contents

# A Note About the Author

Jack London was born in San Francisco in 1876. We think that his name then was John Griffith Chaney. However, Jack's father soon left him and his mother. When Jack was still a baby, his mother married a grocer named John London. Jack's mother was a music teacher. The family lived in Oakland, Pennsylvania. They had very little money.

As a child, Jack loved reading books. He spent a lot of time at his local library. A nice librarian there helped him choose good books.

When Jack was thirteen, he started work. He worked long hours at a factory, putting food in cans. Then he borrowed some money and bought a boat. He used the boat to collect oysters—a kind of seafood—at night. He sold them in the morning. However, after a few months, his boat broke. After that, Jack did more very hard jobs.

At times Jack lived on the streets. He spent some time in prison for this. He also worked as a sailor, and traveled to Japan. When he returned home, he went to Oakland High School. He worked hard and started at the University of California in 1896. However, he had to leave in 1897. That year, he joined in the gold rush to the Klondike River. He did not find any gold, and he became very sick there.

When Jack returned home, he started writing. He wanted to make some money and he had two stories published very quickly. Lots of people were starting to read cheap magazines at that time. Soon Jack started to make a lot of money from his writing.

Jack London married in 1900 and had two daughters. But the marriage was not happy and Jack and his wife got divorced. He married his second wife in 1905. His book *The*

*Call of the Wild* became a big bestseller in 1903. He went on to write *White Fang* in 1906. In his life, he wrote more than fifty books.

By 1913, Jack London was one of the best paid and most widely-read writers in the world. He died in 1916, when he was just forty years old.

# A Note About This Story

This story is about a wolf called White Fang. White Fang was born in the wild, in an area called the Yukon. This area is in the north-west of Canada. There are lots of mountains and rivers in the Yukon and the land is covered with forest. You can travel for hours without seeing people or houses. Winters in the Yukon are very cold and very long. In some areas the ground is frozen all year. Many animals live in the wild there—for example, bears, moose, porcupines, weasels and squirrels, as well as wolves.

*White Fang* was written in 1906. At that time many Indians—native or first peoples—lived in the Yukon. They lived there long before white people. The Indians killed moose and rabbits, and they caught fish. They lived in camps and slept in big tents. The tents were called tepees. The Indians traveled around in long boats called canoes. Or they traveled on sleds pulled by dogs.

In 1886, some people found gold by the Klondike River near Dawson City. When other people heard about this, they all wanted to find gold. So thousands of people came to the Klondike River. This was known as the "gold rush". These people had to travel a long way. They had to make boats to go down the Yukon River to Dawson City. But most people did not find any gold.

White Fang's master, Weedon Scott, was one of these people. He came to the Klondike River from the United States. He knew a lot about mining so he came to help people find gold. But Scott's home was in California, in the United States. California has long, hot summers and many people live there. It is very different from the Yukon.

## The Places in This Story

# A Picture Dictionary

cave

tail

cub

wolf

stomach

paw

hawk

teepees

canoe

riverbank

sled

weasel

lynx

beak

wings

ptarmigan

nest

squirrel

# The People and Animals in This Story

White Fang

Kiche (she-wolf)

Gray Beaver

Beauty Smith

Weedon Scott

Matt

Collie and puppy

# 1

## The Cave in the Riverbank

For many days, the she-wolf and her mate hunted for food together. But after a time, the she-wolf became less interested in hunting. She was looking for something. She spent a lot of time searching under fallen trees. She looked under rocks and in caves in the riverbanks. But she could not find what she wanted.

She was a large wolf—almost five feet long. Her coat was mainly gray, but sometimes it looked a little red. She was getting heavier every day, and she could only run slowly now. Once, when she was running after a rabbit, she suddenly stopped. Then she lay down and rested. Her mate came to her and licked her neck gently. But she growled at him angrily, and he moved away. She was often angry now. But her mate was more patient than ever, and more caring.

Finally the she-wolf found what she was looking for. It was a few miles up a small frozen river. The she-wolf was running behind her mate when she came to the high river bank. She slowed down and walked over to it. There was a small cave in the bank. She went inside it. The entrance to the cave was very small, but inside there was a large round space. It was dry and comfortable. The she-wolf walked around the cave carefully. Then she chose a place in the middle and lay down. She felt pleased and happy.

The she-wolf's mate watched her from the cave's entrance. When she lay down, he wagged his tail from side to side. Then he too lay down in the cave's entrance, and slept.

Outside the cave, the April sun was shining brightly on the snow. Spring was coming, and everything was beginning to grow.

After a while, the she-wolf's mate woke up. He got up and went over to his mate. He wanted her to get up. But she just growled at him. So her mate went out alone into the bright sunshine. He went up the frozen river. The snow was deep and soft, and traveling was difficult. He was gone for eight hours, but he did not find any food. He came back even hungrier.

When he arrived back, he stopped in surprise at the entrance to the cave. There were strange sounds coming from inside. They were not the sounds of his mate. As he moved carefully into the cave, the she-wolf growled. She did not want him near her, so he lay down in the cave's entrance. But he listened to those strange quiet noises for a little while. And soon, the she-wolf's mate fell asleep.

When morning came, the she-wolf's mate heard the strange noises once more. He wanted to see where they were coming from. In the morning light, he could just see five strange little animals. They were lying next to the she-wolf, between her legs. They made tiny crying noises, and their eyes were shut. The she-wolf's mate was surprised.

The she-wolf growled at him. Like all mother wolves, she somehow knew that there was danger. Some father wolves ate their baby cubs. The she-wolf had a strong fear of this. Because of that fear, she would not let her mate near his cubs.

But there was no danger. The she-wolf's mate, too, had a strong feeling. He knew what he had to do. Turning his back on his new-born family, he went out to hunt for meat.

The she-wolf's mate was gone all day. But when he came back, he brought meat for the she-wolf. When she saw this, the she-wolf licked her mate lightly on the neck. She growled at him again when he went near the cubs. But her growl was less angry now. He was doing what a wolf-father should do. And she no longer felt so afraid of him.

———

Four of the cubs all had the slightly red coat of their mother. But one cub was gray, like his father. The gray cub was a fierce little animal—he was strong and ready to fight. His brothers and sisters were, too. After all, their parents and grandparents were meat-killers and meat-eaters. But the gray cub was the fiercest of all the cubs. He growled louder than the others. He was the first one that pushed over another cub with his paw. And he was the first one that pulled at another cub's ear with his teeth.

For the first month of his life, the gray cub spent most of the time sleeping. But soon he could see quite well, and he stayed awake longer. He still drank his mother's milk, but he was starting to eat meat, too. And he was starting to explore his world. The gray cub's world stopped at the walls of the cave. But he soon noticed that one of the walls was different from the others. This was the cave's entrance. Light came from it. The gray cub and his brothers and sisters started to move towards the light. But their mother always pushed them back.

Like most animals of the Wild, the gray cub found out about hunger early in his life. One day there was no more meat. And then, after a time, the cubs found that their mother had no milk left for them. At first, they cried. But mostly they just slept. There were no more little fights, and no more growling. And there was no more moving towards the cave's entrance. The little cubs just slept.

The cubs' father did not know what to do. He traveled a long way looking for food. The she-wolf, too, left her cubs and went out hunting. At last they found meat again. The gray cub started eating, and slowly he came back to life. But he found that his world was different now. He only had one sister left. The other cubs were dead. His little body grew as he ate meat. But for his sister, the food came too late.

Then something else happened. The gray cub no longer saw his father sleeping in the cave's entrance. The gray cub did not know why his father never came back. But the she-wolf did. She followed his smell up the river. It led her past the lynx's lair, or resting place. A little later, she found her mate. He was dead, and there was not much left of his body. But there were many signs of his terrible fight with the lynx.

After that, when the she-wolf went hunting, she never hunted near the lynx's lair. She knew that the lynx was a fierce, angry animal. A pack of wolves could easily frighten a lynx. But for a wolf on its own, lynxes were very dangerous.

12

## 2

# The Wall of Light

For a time, the gray cub no longer went near the cave's entrance. He finally knew from his mother to stay away from it. The feeling of fear was also growing in him. And fear, too, kept him away from the circle of light. When his mother went hunting, he slept most of the time. But when he was awake, he kept very quiet. And he stayed away from the cave's entrance.

But the cub was growing fast. And as he grew, he wanted to learn new things. His mother and fear kept him away from the circle of light for a time. But as he grew, he wanted to explore. One day, when his mother was hunting, he got up and moved towards the cave's entrance.

The light got brighter and brighter. Fear told the gray cub to go back. But he wanted to find out about the world. And so he went on, until suddenly, he arrived at the entrance. The light looked very different now. He could see the trees along the river. Above the trees was a mountain, and above that was a huge sky.

Suddenly the gray cub felt very frightened. The hair stood up on his back, and he growled fiercely at the world. Nothing happened. The gray cub kept looking around. And because he was so interested, he forgot to growl. And he forgot to be afraid. He stepped out bravely into the air, and fell down the riverbank! He hit his nose on the ground and cried out. Then he rolled over and over, down the bank. As he fell, he cried out in fear. At last he reached the bottom of the bank, and stopped rolling. He sat up, crying, and licked the earth off his coat.

Then he looked around. Once again, he forgot about being frightened. There was so much to look at. He nosed around in the grass. He looked at a big plant. Then he walked around a dead pine tree. As he was sniffing at the tree, a squirrel suddenly ran out in front of him. Frightened, the cub put his head down and growled. But the squirrel was even more frightened, and it ran up the tree.

This made the cub feel a little braver. He was learning fast. Some things were alive, and some things were not alive. The things that were not alive did not move. But the things that were alive moved around. And you did not always know what they were going to do next.

The cub decided to explore a little more. He moved slowly at first. He kept knocking his nose against sticks and things. The stones under his feet moved, and it felt very strange to him. But the longer he walked, the better he walked.

He was lucky on his first day out of the cave. Without looking for it, he found meat just outside his cave door. He stepped through a bush and fell into a hidden ptarmigan nest. He sat up and found himself looking at seven baby ptarmigans. They were making a lot of noise, and he felt frightened at first. But then he saw that they were very small. He felt braver. He put his paw on one of the baby birds, and it moved around. He smelled it, and picked it up in his mouth. And suddenly he felt very hungry. He closed his teeth, and warm blood ran in his mouth. It felt good. So he ate the ptarmigans one by one.

As he came out of the bush, he suddenly heard a loud noise. The mother ptarmigan ran towards him and started hitting him with her wings. At first he hid his head between his paws and cried. Then he got angry. He bit into one of her wings, and pulled. The ptarmigan pulled back, still hitting the cub with her other wing. The cub felt excited. This was his first fight. This live thing was meat, and he wanted to kill it.

He held onto the wing, growling between his teeth. The ptarmigan kept screaming and hitting him with her free wing. Then at last she stopped moving. The cub and the ptarmigan lay on the ground and looked at each other. Then the ptarmigan pecked the cub's nose with her beak. He pulled back, still holding on to the bird's wing. She pecked him again and again. Suddenly the cub forgot the excitement of the fight. Crying, he at last let go of the ptarmigan. He turned around quickly and ran across to some bushes. There he lay down to rest, his nose still hurting.

But as he lay there, the gray cub was suddenly frightened once more. He could feel that something terrible was going to happen. He felt a rush of air on his face. Then a large hawk flew silently down and took hold of the ptarmigan. The ptarmigan screamed with fear as the hawk carried it up into the sky.

The cub lay in the bushes for a long time. He had learned many things that day. Live things were meat. They were good to eat. But live things could also hurt. The cub suddenly felt very tired. And he remembered his mother. At that moment, he wanted her more than anything else in the world. So he started to look for the cave.

But as the cub was walking along between some bushes, he suddenly heard an angry cry. Then a weasel appeared out of the bushes. The weasel's loud cry made the cub's hair stand up, and he growled at her. She came closer and closer. Then suddenly she jumped at him, biting into his throat.

At first the cub growled and tried to fight. But his growl became a frightened little cry. He did not want to fight any more, he just wanted to get away. But the weasel held on hard, pressing down with her teeth.

The gray cub was lucky that day. Suddenly the she-wolf came running through the bushes. The weasel let go of the cub and bit into the she-wolf's throat. But the she-wolf threw her head back, shaking the weasel off. The weasel flew up into the air, and the she-wolf caught it in her mouth. She pressed her teeth down hard, and the weasel was dead.

The cub was very happy to find his mother. But the she-wolf was even more pleased to see him. She licked the cuts in his neck. Together, they ate the weasel. Then they went back to the cave to sleep.

# 3

# The Man-animals

After his first adventures, the cub started to learn quickly. Every day he went a little further away from home. But when he was tired, he found his way back to the cave. He was starting to understand how strong he was. And he was starting to know when he should be careful. He no longer fell over or walked into things. Now he moved like his mother, quickly and silently.

His need to kill was getting stronger every day. He realized now how powerful his mother was. She always brought him meat, and she was afraid of nothing. He felt her power in other ways, too. Now, when she was angry with him, she bit him with her teeth. He had to do what she wanted. And the older he grew, the fiercer she became.

After a while, the cub started to hunt with his mother. He watched her kill meat. Slowly he became braver, and was no longer afraid of little things. He was learning the law of meat: EAT, OR BE EATEN. He knew that he did not have to worry about some animals. They were too small to kill him. But other animals were more dangerous. And if he did not kill them, they would certainly kill him.

The cub had many things to learn. The world was full of surprises for him. But he loved to feel the life inside himself. Running after meat made him feel excited and he enjoyed fighting. And after a hunt, he loved to lie in the sun, full of food. He was very much alive, very happy, and very proud of himself.

One day, however, life suddenly changed. The cub ran down to the river to drink early one morning. He was still sleepy, so at first he did not notice anything. Then, suddenly, he saw and smelled something strange. Five strange animals were sitting in front of him. The cub had never seen men before, and suddenly he felt very small.

The cub knew nothing about men. But his parents and grandparents knew about men. They knew men were more powerful than any other living thing. And somehow the cub could feel that, too.

The men were Indians. One of them walked over to him. Then slowly the man reached down to pick him up. The cub's hair stood up on his back, and he showed his little teeth.

"Look at his white fangs!" the man laughed. The man's hand came closer and closer. Then the cub suddenly bit the man's hand. At once, the man hit him on the head, and the cub fell onto his side. Suddenly the cub forgot all about fighting. He sat up and cried.

The four men laughed even more loudly. And the cub cried even more. But in the middle of his crying, he suddenly heard something. He gave one last long cry. Then he stopped his noise and waited for his mother. His mother killed everything and was never afraid. She was fierce and powerful. And she was coming.

She was growling as she ran towards him. She knew his cry, and she was running to save him. The cub ran towards

*"Look at his fangs!" the man laughed.*

her. The men stepped back a little, and the she-wolf growled at them fiercely.

"Kiche!" one of the men suddenly cried in surprise. "Kiche!" And the fearless she-wolf sank slowly to the ground. The cub could not understand. Once again, he felt the strong power of man.

The man who spoke came over to Kiche. He put his hand on her head, and she just sank down lower. She did not bite or growl. The other men came closer, too.

"She ran away a year ago, didn't she, Gray Beaver?" said one of the men.

"Yes," Gray Beaver answered. "There was nothing to eat."

"She has lived with the wolves," another man said.

"It is not surprising," said Gray Beaver. "Her father was a wolf. And now she has a cub. His teeth are white, so I will call him White Fang. And he will be my dog."

The cub watched as the man-animals talked to each other. Then Gray Beaver took a stick and some string and tied Kiche to a tree. White Fang followed.

After a time, White Fang heard strange noises coming nearer. A few minutes later, about forty men, women and children came walking down the track. They were carrying things for their camp. There were many dogs, too, carrying bags on their backs. As soon as the dogs saw the cub and his mother, they ran towards them. White Fang was knocked down, and he felt teeth bite into his body.

But after just a few seconds, he was up again. The man-animals were fighting the dogs away with sticks and stones.

White Fang licked his cuts. This was his first meeting with the man-animals' dogs. He was not happy that they attacked him. And he was not happy that his mother was tied up. He needed to be with his mother. And this meant that he too was not free.

At that moment, the man-animals got up and started walking. One of them untied Kiche from the tree and took her with him. White Fang followed behind her, feeling worried and frightened by this new adventure.

# 4

## The Camp

The men and their dogs went a long way down the little river, and Kiche and White Fang followed. At last they arrived at the big Mackenzie River. Here they stopped, and began putting up their tepees. White Fang watched. Soon around him were great tall tepees. He could not see the mountains or the river any more. He could only see tepees.

White Fang was frightened of the tepees at first. But he watched women and children going in and out of them. He saw other dogs trying to get into them, too. And his fear quickly disappeared.

Kiche was tied up at the camp once more. At first White Fang stayed by her side, but after a while he went to look around. Soon a puppy came towards him. The young dog did not seem dangerous and White Fang wanted to be friendly. But the puppy, whose name was Lip-lip, was not friendly. He liked frightening other puppies so he showed his teeth when he saw White Fang. They walked around each other, growling.

Then suddenly, Lip-lip jumped forward and bit White Fang's shoulder. White Fang cried out in pain. He tried to bite back at Lip-lip. But Lip-lip had fought many fights. He bit White Fang again and again. At last, White Fang ran crying back to his mother.

Kiche licked White Fang's cuts. She wanted him to stay with her. But he was too interested in everything around him. So a few minutes later he went away again. This time he saw Gray Beaver doing something with sticks. Women and children were bringing more sticks to the Indian. White Fang went closer and watched. Suddenly he saw a color like the sun in the sticks. White Fang knew nothing about fire. He moved forwards towards it. He touched it with his nose and put his tongue into it.

For a moment he could not move. Then he ran back, crying out in pain. It was the worst hurt he had ever known. He tried to lick his nose, but his tongue was burnt, too. He cried and cried. But Gray Beaver and the other animals laughed. And the more White Fang cried, the more they laughed at him.

Suddenly White Fang did not want them to laugh at him

anymore. Their laughter was hurting him as much as the fire. He turned and ran back to Kiche.

That night, White Fang lay awake by his mother's side. His nose and tongue were hurting, but he was worried about something else. He wanted to be in his old home. He wanted the quiet of the river and the little cave. Here, the dogs were always fighting and the man-animals were always moving around. It was too noisy. White Fang wanted his old home in the riverbank.

————

In his first days at the camp, White Fang ran around exploring. He was learning more and more about the man-animals. He was learning how powerful they were. Like his mother, Kiche, White Fang was beginning to do what they wanted. When they walked towards him, he moved out of their way. When they called him, he came. When they told him to go, he ran away quickly. He knew that he had to please the man-animals. When he did not please them, they hit him.

White Fang learned quickly about life in the camp. He learned that the women were kinder than the men. He learned that the children liked to throw stones at the dogs.

Lip-lip made White Fang's life in the camp difficult. Every time White Fang left his mother's side, Lip-lip followed him. And as soon as there were no man-animals near, Lip-lip started a fight. Lip-lip won the fight every time, so he enjoyed it very much.

But although White Fang hated the fights with Lip-lip, he was not frightened. He was already a fierce little cub, but he became even fiercer. White Fang could not play with the other puppies in the camp because of Lip-lip. As soon as White Fang came near the puppies, Lip-lip fought with him. So White Fang grew up quickly. He could not play, so he became clever instead. He learned to find meat and fish in the camp. He watched everything and listened to everything. And he learned to stay away from Lip-lip.

At last, one day, Gray Beaver untied Kiche. White Fang was very excited. He went happily with her around the camp. And because he was with his mother, Lip-lip stayed away from him.

Later that day, Kiche and White Fang went close to the woods by the camp. Kiche stopped as they got closer, but White Fang went on. He wanted his mother to come with him. He ran back to her and licked her face. Then he ran on again. But she did not move. She could hear the call of the Wild too. But she could also hear a louder call—the call of man. After a while, Kiche turned and walked slowly back towards the camp.

White Fang sat down by a tree and cried quietly. He could smell the pine trees, and he was remembering his life in the Wild. But he was still a puppy. The call of his mother was stronger than the call of the Wild. So after a moment, he got up and walked slowly after her.

In the Wild, an animal never has a long time with its mother. But for White Fang, the men made the time even shorter. Gray Beaver sold Kiche to another man, who was going away up the River Mackenzie. When the man put Kiche into his canoe, White Fang tried to follow her. The man pushed him away, and set off up the river. But White Fang jumped into the water and swam after them. He could hear Gray Beaver shouting at him to come back.

Then Gray Beaver got into his canoe, and went after White Fang. He pulled the cub out of the water, and hit him hard, again and again. White Fang cried out in pain. Even when Gray Beaver stopped hitting him, White Fang went on crying. The man threw him down into the bottom of the

*Then Gray Beaver got into his canoe, and went after White Fang.*

canoe, and kicked him. Suddenly White Fang bit hard into Gray Beaver's foot.

This time Gray Beaver hit White Fang even harder than before. White Fang thought it was bad the first time. But this time, it was terrible. When Gray Beaver threw him down in the boat again, his little body hurt all over. And when Gray Beaver kicked him again, White Fang did not bite. He knew now that he must never bite a man-animal.

When the boat arrived back at the riverbank, Gray Beaver threw White Fang onto the grass. The cub pulled himself up, shaking and crying. Lip-lip was standing on the river bank, watching. He jumped onto White Fang, biting into him with his teeth. But Gray Beaver kicked Lip-lip away. When their animals did something wrong, the man-animals hurt them. But they did not let other animals hurt them too.

That night, when everything was quiet, White Fang remembered his mother. He cried so loudly that he woke up Gray Beaver. And Gray Beaver hit him again. After that, he only cried quietly when the man-animals were near. But sometimes, he went off to the edge of the woods by himself. And then he cried out loud.

He wanted to run away back into the Wild. But he hoped his mother would come back to the camp. So he had to wait for her. And he was not unhappy. He was learning how to get along with Gray Beaver. He learned to do exactly what Gray Beaver told him. And then he did not get hurt. Sometimes Gray Beaver even threw White Fang a piece of meat. That made him feel happy. Gray Beaver never spoke kindly to White Fang. He never stroked his back. But White Fang was starting to like the man-animal. Although he did not know it, he was also starting to like camp life.

# 5

# The Enemy of the Pack

Because Lip-lip made his life so difficult, White Fang became fiercer than ever. Whenever there was trouble in the camp, it was usually because of White Fang. All the young dogs followed Lip-lip and turned against White Fang. White Fang fought with them all. As soon as a fight started, all the young dogs joined in. Together, they all attacked White Fang.

Because he always had to fight with the whole pack of dogs, White Fang learned two important things. First, he learned how to take care of himself when the pack attacked him. He learned that he must always stay on his feet. The older dogs pushed him backwards or sideways with their heavy bodies. But he always kept his feet on the ground.

The other thing White Fang learned was to fight quickly. As soon as White Fang started fighting with one dog, all the other young dogs came to fight him. So White Fang learned to attack as fast and hard as possible. Most dogs growled before they started fighting. But White Fang learned to attack without any warning. He attacked before the other dog knew what was happening. He rushed in, biting shoulders and ears. Then he easily knocked the dog down.

When a dog was knocked off its feet, it showed its throat for a moment. And you could kill an animal by biting at its throat. White Fang knew this. He knew it from all the hunting wolves before him. He was still young. His mouth was not big enough or strong enough to kill with one bite yet. But many of the dogs in the camp had cuts on their throat from White Fang. One day, he caught a dog on its own. White Fang knocked the dog over and bit at its throat, killing it. That night, there were many angry people in the camp. They knew White Fang was the killer. But Gray Beaver kept White Fang in his tepee, and did not let anybody inside.

———

In December, Gray Beaver went traveling up the Mackenzie river. His son, Mit-sah, went with him, and he drove a sled pulled by seven puppies. White Fang was a good sled dog. He worked hard. And he always did what the man-animals told him.

But the other puppies all knew that they had to be careful of White Fang. If they ate their meat too slowly, he stole it. If he walked among them, they had to get out of his way. And if they growled at him, he attacked them. Then they had no chance. They were hurt before they even started fighting.

White Fang traveled with Gray Beaver for many months. Pulling the sled made him grow stronger and stronger. He was growing up fast. And he thought he knew the world well now. His world was a fierce world. There was no warmth in his world, no friendship or gladness.

But White Fang was also learning that there was an agreement between dog and man. Gray Beaver gave him food and fire, and took care of him. And White Fang worked for Gray Beaver, pulling the sled. He also guarded Gray Beaver's things. If anyone came near Gray Beaver's tepee, White Fang bit them. He knew that he had to do this. But he did not do it for love. He did not understand what love was.

In April, Gray Beaver and White Fang returned to the home camp. White Fang was now a year old. Next to Lip-lip, he was the largest puppy in the camp. He was tall and strong, and his coat was wolf-gray. White Fang walked around the camp, feeling stronger and older than before. Many of the older dogs were not as big as he remembered. He felt less frightened of them now.

One day, White Fang was walking around the camp when he saw Kiche. He stopped and looked at her. Then she growled at him, and suddenly he remembered. All his old feelings came rushing back. He ran towards her happily, but she growled again and bit him. He could not understand it.

But Kiche did not remember White Fang. She had new cubs now, and she was taking care of them. One of the cubs came up to White Fang. He sniffed at it. And Kiche immediately jumped at him and bit him again. White Fang moved away. He did not fight female dogs. That was a law among dogs and wolves. It was something that they knew without understanding why. White Fang watched Kiche licking her puppy. And suddenly all his feelings for her died. There was no place for her in his life now. And there was no place for him in hers.

When White Fang was two, there was a terrible famine. First, in the summer, there was little fish. And in the winter, there were no large animals for hunting. There were no rabbits either, and the hunting animals died. Weak with hunger, they ate each other. In the camp, the old and weak died. The camp was full of crying. Women and children went hungry so that the men—the hunters—could have a little food. The men went through the forest looking for meat every day, but came home with nothing.

The man-animals were so hungry that they ate their shoes and their gloves. They ate the dogs too, and the dogs ate each other. The strongest and bravest dogs left the camp and ran away to the woods. There they were eaten by wolves, or they died of hunger.

In these terrible times, White Fang, too, ran away into the woods. He knew about living in the Wild, so he survived better than most of the dogs. He became very good at catching small animals. He watched squirrels for hours, and then attacked them at just the right moment. He dug wood-mice out of the ground, and fought with weasels. And he went quietly back to the camp and stole rabbits from the man-animals.

White Fang was lucky in the Wild. He always found something to kill when he was getting really hungry. And when he was weak, nothing found him. One day he met a pack of hungry wolves. But he was strong from eating a lynx. The wolves ran after him for a long way. But White Fang was faster than them, and he was able to escape.

After that, White Fang traveled back to the area where he was born. He rested for a while in the empty lair of the old lynx. In the last days of the famine, White Fang met Lip-lip, who was also living in the woods. They stopped when they saw each other. The hair on White Fang's back went up, and he growled fiercely. He was having a good week, and he was full of food. He jumped straight at Lip-lip, knocking him down. Then he bit into the dog's throat until he died.

One day soon after, White Fang found a new man-animal camp at the edge of a forest. He watched carefully from the woods for a while. Soon he understood that it was the old camp, but in a new place. But it was different now. There was no crying. He could hear happy noises, and he could smell fish. There was food. The famine was gone. White Fang quickly found Gray Beaver's tepee and ran straight into it. Gray Beaver was not there, but his wife was pleased to see White Fang. She gave him some fish, and he lay down to wait for Gray Beaver.

# 6

# *At Fort Yukon*

When White Fang was nearly five years old, Gray Beaver took him on another long journey. They traveled down the Mackenzie River, and across the mountains to the Yukon River. They stayed in many camps along the way. At each place White Fang brought terrible trouble. He was such a fierce animal. As soon as a dog growled at him, White Fang jumped at its throat.

After several months, Gray Beaver and White Fang arrived at Fort Yukon. And there they stopped. There were many Indians there, and a lot of excitement. It was the summer of 1898. Thousands of gold-hunters were going up the Yukon River to Dawson and the Klondike. The hunters were looking for gold and many of them stopped at Fort Yukon on their way. They rested there, and bought things for their journey.

Gray Beaver knew about the gold rush, and he had with him a lot of shoes, gloves and furs—animal coats. Everyone wanted to buy them and Gray Beaver made a lot of money.

At Fort Yukon, White Fang saw white men for the first time. Every few days, a big boat arrived and stopped there for a while. There were many white men on the boats. And many of them came from a long way away. They stopped at Fort Yukon for a while. Then they sailed up the river on the boats again.

White Fang quickly found that the white men's dogs were weak. None of them knew how to fight. And because White Fang now hated all dogs, he attacked them all. When the dogs came off the boats, they ran at him. To them, he was a wolf. He was the Wild. And because they had a great fear of the Wild, they wanted to attack him. But he always jumped to the side. Then he knocked them down, and bit their throats. After that, the Indian dogs jumped on the white men's dogs and tore them to pieces. White Fang was clever. He knew that the man-animals got angry when their dogs were killed. He always started an attack, but he let the pack of Indian dogs kill the white men's dogs. Then the white men rushed in, hitting the dogs. And White Fang just stood nearby, watching.

One white man took out his gun when his dog was killed. He killed six Indian dogs from the pack. White Fang enjoyed it all. Gray Beaver was busy selling things, and there was no work for White Fang. So he stayed waiting for boats all day.

There were a few white men living in Fort Yukon. They did not like the new white men who came off the boats every day. So they liked seeing White Fang and the Indian dogs attack the travelers' dogs. When a boat arrived, they often came down to the river. They enjoyed watching the dog fights.

But one man enjoyed the fights more than anyone else. He came running as soon as he heard a boat arrive. He watched all the fights. And sometimes, when a dog was killed, he jumped into the air in excitement. Best of all, this man liked watching White Fang. He saw how clever Gray Beaver's dog was.

This man was called "Beauty" by the other men. He worked as a cook at the fort. The men called him Beauty as a joke, because he was certainly not beautiful. He was a small man, with a large, heavy mouth. He had big yellow teeth and dirty yellow eyes. On some parts of his head he had lots of hair, and on others he had none.

Beauty Smith was a horrible-looking man. He was also often very angry. As soon as Beauty Smith saw White Fang, he wanted him. He tried to make friends with the wolf, but White Fang just growled. White Fang did not like Beauty Smith. He could feel that this man was bad.

One day, Beauty Smith came to Gray Beaver's camp. As soon as White Fang heard the man coming, he growled. Then he walked away to the other side of the camp. He did not want to be near Beauty Smith.

Beauty Smith wanted to buy White Fang. But Gray Beaver would not sell him. The Indian had a lot of money now, and he did not need any more. White Fang was a very strong sled-dog. He was leader of the sled pack. He was a great leader and a great fighter. Gray Beaver did not want to sell him.

*As soon as Beauty Smith saw White Fang, he wanted him.*

But Beauty Smith kept coming to the camp. He started bringing whiskey—a strong alcoholic drink—when he came to see Gray Beaver. The more whiskey Gray Beaver drank, the more he wanted. He spent more and more of his money on whiskey. At last his money was all gone. Once more, Beauty Smith asked about buying White Fang. This time, he said he would pay Gray Beaver with bottles of whiskey. And this time Gray Beaver said yes.

White Fang did not want to go with Beauty Smith. When the man came to take him away, he jumped at him. He tried to bite him. Beauty Smith put a leather strap around his neck. Then he hit White Fang with a stick until he followed him back to his home. But as soon as Beauty Smith went to bed, White Fang bit quickly through the strap. Then he walked back to Gray Beaver's camp. He did not have an agreement with Beauty Smith. He was Gray Beaver's dog, not Beauty Smith's.

In the morning, Beauty Smith came to take White Fang away again. First, he gave White Fang a beating—he hit him again and again. He hit him much harder than Gray Beaver. Beauty Smith enjoyed hitting White Fang. His eyes lit up as he heard the dog's cries of pain. Beauty Smith had no power among other men. So he enjoyed having power over animals that were weaker than himself.

Once again, Beauty Smith took White Fang home. This time he tied him up with a stick. But once again, White Fang bit through the stick that he was tied up with. And once again he went back to Gray Beaver. When Beauty Smith came back to get White Fang, he hit him even harder than before. When Beauty Smith stopped hitting him, White Fang was sick. He could not walk at first, and Beauty Smith had to wait. But at last, weak and shaking, White Fang followed the white man back to his home.

This time, Beauty Smith tied White Fang with a metal chain. Again and again, White Fang tried to pull the chain from the wall. But even he could not free himself this time.

After a few days, Gray Beaver set off back to the Mackenzie, with no money and no dog. White Fang stayed at Fort Yukon. He had a new master now—he was another man's dog. And this master was more like an animal than a man.

# 7
# *The Fighting Wolf*

As Beauty Smith's dog, White Fang became fierce and terrible. He was kept on a chain, fenced inside a small pen.

Beauty Smith enjoyed making White Fang angry. White Fang hated it when people laughed at him. Beauty Smith quickly learned that laughing at White Fang made him go crazy. When Beauty Smith laughed at him, White Fang became wild with anger.

White Fang already hated all other dogs. Now he started to hate everything. He hated the chain he was kept on. He hated the men who looked in at him through the fence. He hated the fence. And most of all, he hated this terrible man-animal, Beauty Smith.

But Beauty Smith knew what he was doing. One day, a group of men came to stand outside White Fang's pen. Beauty Smith came into the pen and took the chain off White Fang's neck. At once, White Fang started to run around the pen. He looked fierce and terrible. He was a big dog now, and heavier than a wolf. He was stronger than ever.

Suddenly the door of the pen opened again. Then a big dog was pushed into the pen, and the door was shut. White Fang did not wait for a moment. He was full of hate, and ready to fight with anything. He jumped straight at the dog, and bit his neck. The dog jumped back at White Fang. But White Fang was too fast for him. Every time the other dog jumped at him, White Fang moved quickly away. But White Fang bit the other dog again and again.

At last a man came and took the other dog out of the pen. White Fang was the winner of the fight. And Beauty Smith won a lot of money from the men watching the fight.

After that, there were many more fights. White Fang started to look forward to them. He won every fight. One day he fought against a wolf from the Wild. Another day he fought against two dogs at the same time. It was his hardest fight. He killed the other two dogs, but he was half-killed himself.

In the winter, Beauty Smith took White Fang on a boat up the Yukon River to Dawson. White Fang was kept in a metal cage. Lots of people knew about White Fang now and many men came to look at him. They tried to make him growl. They laughed at him. These men made White Fang fiercer than ever.

When he was with Gray Beaver, White Fang was always careful of a man with a stick. He did what the man wanted. But Beauty Smith made White Fang go crazy. Whenever White Fang saw Beauty Smith, he became full of anger and hate. He growled and jumped up at his cage. Even after Beauty Smith hit White Fang, he still growled at him. White Fang never stopped growling at Beauty Smith.

In Dawson, White Fang was kept in his cage. Men paid money to look at him. He also had fights in Dawson. The fights went on until one of the dogs died. And White Fang always won. He never let any animal knock him off his feet. He was fast, and he jumped in without any warning.

Then, one day, a man came to the Klondike with a bull-dog. Bull-dogs are small but very strong. This dog was also a very famous fighter. Beauty Smith and his friends all wanted the bull-dog to fight with White Fang. The week before the fight, they were very excited. They talked about nothing else.

At last the day of the big fight came. The bull-dog was pushed into White Fang's pen, and White Fang looked at it for a moment. It was different from other dogs. It was short and fat and it moved in a strange way.

"Go on, Cherokee!" the men watching shouted. "Eat him up!"

But Cherokee, the bull-dog, just looked around happily, wagging his short tail. Then White Fang jumped in and bit his neck. The bull-dog did not seem hurt. It did not even growl. It just turned and followed after White Fang. Again and again White Fang jumped in and bit the bull-dog. But the strange dog just kept following him. White Fang was confused. The dog did not have any hair, and he could bite it easily. But it never growled or cried out.

Cherokee was confused, too. He usually fought close with other dogs. But White Fang never came close. He jumped in and out. He kept biting, but he never held on.

After a while, Cherokee's ears were torn to pieces by White Fang. The bull-dog's neck and shoulders were covered in cuts. He was even bleeding from his mouth. But White Fang could not reach Cherokee's throat. The bull-dog was too short, and his mouth was too big. White Fang could not knock the bull-dog off his feet, either.

Then a chance came. Cherokee turned his head away for a moment, and White Fang jumped at his shoulder. But the bull-dog was very short and White Fang fell across him. For the first time ever in a fight, White Fang fell on his side. At that moment, the bull-dog took hold of his throat.

White Fang jumped around wildly. He was trying to shake off the bull-dog. He hated feeling its hold on him. It made him go crazy. But Cherokee would not let go. The bull-dog's feet hardly touched the ground. His body flew around. But he held on hard to White Fang's neck. White Fang ran around and around. He turned and moved backwards. But he could not shake the bull-dog off.

At last, tired, White Fang stopped. He could not understand. Other dogs did not fight like this. While White Fang was quiet, Cherokee took his chance. Still holding on, he moved his mouth a little closer to White Fang's throat. White Fang was on his back now. Bit by bit, Cherokee took more of White Fang's neck into his mouth. White Fang was finding it harder and harder to breathe.

The fight was almost over. Beauty Smith came into the pen and stood laughing at White Fang. He knew that White Fang hated that. At once, White Fang went crazy with anger. He got up to his feet, even though the bull-dog was still biting his neck. But he could hardly move around the pen. He kept trying to shake the bull-dog from his neck. At last he fell backwards.

"Cherokee! Cherokee!" the men outside cried. The bull-dog wagged its tail, still holding tight to White Fang's throat.

At that moment, the men heard voices coming close. They looked up, afraid of the police. But they saw two men with a sled and dogs. The strange men stopped their dogs near the pen. Then they came to look. They wanted to know what was happening.

By then, White Fang was not moving much any more. He could hardly breathe. Beauty Smith could see that the fight was almost lost. He jumped up and ran into the pen. Then he started kicking White Fang.

But someone else followed Beauty Smith into the pen. It was one of the men from the sled. He was a tall young man and his face was red from the cold air. As Beauty Smith kicked White Fang, the young man hit him in the face. Beauty Smith fell backwards into the snow.

Then the young man turned to the men outside the pen. "You animals!" he shouted at them.

Beauty Smith was on his feet. But the young man hit him again. Again Beauty Smith fell back into the snow. But this time he lay there, and did not get up.

The other man from the sled was coming into the pen.

"Come on, Matt," the tall young man said. "Help me."

Both men bent over the dogs. Matt held onto White Fang, and the tall young man tried to pull the bull-dog's mouth open.

"Those men are animals!" he cried angrily every time he pulled. But the bull-dog would not let go.

"It's no good, Mr Scott," said Matt at last. "You can't pull them apart like that. You need to put something in its mouth. Then perhaps you can push it open."

Scott put his hand in his pocket. He took out his gun, and put it in Cherokee's mouth. Then, slowly, he started to push the dog's mouth open with the gun. With one last push, he opened Cherokee's mouth, and the dogs were pulled apart.

"Take your dog!" Scott shouted at Cherokee's master, who was standing in the pen. The man pulled Cherokee outside.

White Fang tried to get up. But his legs were too weak, and he fell back into the snow. His eyes were half-closed, and his mouth was open. Matt looked at him carefully.

"He's almost finished," he said. "But he's still breathing."

Beauty Smith was on his feet again. He came over to look at White Fang. Scott turned to him angrily. He took out some money.

"Here you are, you animal," he said to Beauty Smith. "I'm going to take your dog from you. And I'll give you a hundred and fifty dollars for him."

Beauty Smith put his hands behind his back and shook his head.

"I'm not selling," he said.

"Oh yes, you are," said Scott. "Because I'm buying.

Here's your money. The dog's mine. Are you going to take the money? Or do I have to hit you again?"

"I'll go to the police when I get back to Dawson," said Beauty Smith.

"If you do, I'll have you sent out of town," said Scott. "Do you understand?"

Beauty Smith did not say anything. He made a noise through his nose.

"Do you understand?" Scott shouted fiercely. His hand was up, ready to hit Beauty Smith again.

"Yes," said Beauty Smith quietly, moving backwards.

The men outside the pen laughed at him.

"Careful, Beauty! He might bite you!" someone shouted.

Scott and Matt turned back to look at White Fang.

"Who is that?" one of the men asked, pointing at Scott.

"Weedon Scott," said another. "He's a mining expert—he knows all about mining. He's friends with all the important people in town. You don't want to make trouble with him."

# 8

# *Weedon Scott*

"It's no good," said Weedon Scott, looking at White Fang. "He's a wolf. We'll never be able to control or tame him."

"I don't agree," said Matt. "I think he's probably got a bit of dog in him. And he's been tamed before. Look at the marks on his stomach. He was a sled-dog before Beauty Smith found him."

Scott looked closer at White Fang.

"You're right, Matt!" he said. "Well, I never!"

Then he shook his head.

"But we've had him for two weeks already. And he's even wilder now than he was then."

"Why don't we let him off his chain for a bit?" said Matt. "Give him a chance."

Holding a stick, Matt walked slowly up to White Fang. White Fang watched the stick carefully, growling. Then Matt took the chain off and stepped back. White Fang did not know what to do. He had been tied up for months. Beauty Smith only ever let him off the chain for fights. He walked a little way away, watching the two men all the time.

Scott went into his cabin—a small wooden house—and brought out a piece of meat for White Fang. But when he threw it, one of the other dogs immediately jumped at it.

"No, Major!" Matt shouted out. But it was too late. As soon as Major bit into the meat, White Fang jumped at him. Major fell to the ground, bleeding from his throat. Matt kicked White Fang, and at once White Fang bit him in the leg.

"He bit me!" shouted Matt, looking down at his bleeding leg.

"I told you it was no good, Matt," said Scott. "I didn't want to do this. But it's the only thing we can do."

He was taking out his gun.

"Don't kill him, Mr Scott," said Matt. "That dog has had a terrible time. Give him a chance."

"But he's killed one of our dogs. And look at your leg!"

Scott took up his gun, and at once White Fang started growling.

"Wait, Mr Scott! Look at that!" cried Matt. "He's a smart dog. He knows what a gun is."

"Well, I never!" said Scott. He put his gun down. At once, White Fang stopped growling.

"Let's see what happens now," said Matt, taking his own gun out.

He lifted it slowly to his shoulder, and White Fang growled more and more. When the gun was pointing straight at White Fang, he jumped behind the cabin. Matt put the gun down slowly.

"We can't kill that dog, Mr Scott," he said. "He's too smart."

———

The next day, Weedon Scott sat down near White Fang and spoke softly. White Fang growled. He was waiting for a beating. But the man did not have a stick. And his voice gave White Fang a strange, safe feeling.

After a long time, the man brought out some meat. He held it out in his hand, but White Fang would not take it. At last, the man threw the meat on the snow. White Fang took the meat in his mouth, but he was watching the man all the time. The man threw some more bits of meat, and White Fang ate them. But the man held the next bit in his hand. He would not throw it.

White Fang was hungry, and it was good meat. Very slowly, he moved closer to the man's hand. He watched the man all the time, growling. Then at last he ate the meat. Nothing happened. He ate some more meat from the man's hand. And there was still no beating.

The man kept talking. There was kindness in his voice. Now the man's hand moved closer and closer to his head. White Fang growled. Slowly the hand stroked his head. Then it rubbed his ears. It felt wrong to White Fang. He was ready for the man to hit him at any moment. But it did not hurt. In fact, White Fang liked the feeling.

———

It was a new beginning for White Fang, and the end of his old life of hate. Weedon Scott was touching some feelings deep inside the wolf. They were feelings that were almost dead. One of these feelings was love. But the love only came slowly. It started with *liking*. White Fang did not run away, because he liked Weedon Scott. He knew that he needed a master. And he liked this master much better than Beauty Smith.

White Fang made it his job to guard Scott's cabin. He walked around it at night while the sled-dogs slept. And he jumped at anyone who came near.

Every day, Scott gave White Fang kindness. Every day he stroked him and rubbed his ears. White Fang always growled when Scott stroked him. But slowly the sound of the growl started to change. There was a little bit of happiness in it, which only Scott could hear. White Fang started to love his master. When Scott was at home he felt full of happiness. But when his master was away, he felt empty. White Fang did not show these feelings. He never ran to meet his master. He never jumped up at Scott when he came home. But White Fang was always waiting for his master and looking out for him. And when Scott was home, he watched him all the time. His master gave him love, and he gave it back.

White Fang fought with the other dogs at first. But they quickly learned to move out of his way. If they did what he wanted, he left them alone.

White Fang started working for Matt as a sled-dog. He was the smartest dog and the strongest dog. So he quickly became the leader of the pack. But although he worked at the sled all day, he did not stop guarding his master's cabin at night.

"I have to say," Matt said one day, "you were a smart man to take that dog from Beauty Smith."

But in the spring, a terrible thing happened to White Fang. Scott went away traveling. White Fang did not understand where his master was. The first night, he waited outside in the cold for his master all night. But no master came. Days went by, and still the master did not come back. White Fang became sick. He would not work and he would not eat. When the other dogs jumped at him, he did not fight back. Matt brought him into the cabin, and he just lay on the floor near the fire. He was not interested in anything.

Then one night, he suddenly got up from the floor and looked at the door. He stood there listening carefully. A moment later, Weedon Scott walked in. White Fang did not rush towards him like the other dogs. But when Scott came over to him, he wagged his tail. Then he put his head under his master's arm and growled with happiness.

"Well, I never!" laughed Matt.

White Fang quickly got better. He stayed in the cabin for another two nights. Then he went back outside. When he came out of the cabin, the other dogs jumped at him. They forgot that he was stronger than them.

"Go on, wolf!" said Matt.

White Fang was full of life once more. He jumped back at them, and they ran away, frightened. They did not come back until after dark. And this time, they remembered that White Fang was their leader.

———

When Scott started getting ready for another journey, White Fang understood at once. Every night, the men heard him outside the door of the cabin, crying quietly.

"He knows that you're going," said Matt.

"I can't take a wolf to California," replied Scott.

"I'm not sure what he'll do without you," said Matt.

"Stop it!" shouted Scott. "I've made up my mind."

"Of course you have," said Matt with a smile.

A few days later, White Fang saw Scott packing things into a big bag. Now he was sure that his master was going. That night, he pointed his nose at the moon and howled with sadness.

Inside the cabin, the two men heard his cries.

"He's not eating again," said Matt.

Weedon Scott said nothing.

"I hope he doesn't die this time," Matt went on.

"Stop it, Matt!" Scott shouted. "I can't take him with me. You know that."

The next day, White Fang followed his master everywhere. Two men arrived and took Scott's bags away. Then Scott called White Fang inside the cabin.

"You poor old thing," he said, rubbing White Fang's ears. "I've got to go away, old man, and you can't come with me. Now give me a growl—a goodbye growl."

But White Fang wouldn't growl. He put his head under his master's arm.

"Hurry up, the boat's going soon!" Matt called.

"Come on!"

47

As the two men left the cabin, they could hear White Fang crying inside.

"Take care of him, Matt," Scott said, as they walked down to the river. "Write to me and tell me how he is."

White Fang's cry was full of terrible sadness.

Down at the river, the boat was full of people. It was the first boat of the year. Everyone wanted to get away from the mines. Matt came onto the boat and stood saying goodbye to Scott. But as he turned to go, his mouth suddenly fell open. He was looking at something on the boat behind Scott. Scott turned around. Sitting a little way away was White Fang.

"Well, I never!" said Scott. "Did you lock the cabin door?"

"I certainly did," replied Matt. "I'll take him with me. Come here, boy!"

Matt moved towards White Fang, but White Fang ran away from him. He disappeared between the legs of a group of men. But when Scott called, White Fang came to him at once. Scott stroked White Fang, and then looked closer at his face. There were cuts on his nose and around his eyes.

"He jumped through the window!" cried Matt, touching White Fang's stomach. "His stomach is covered in cuts."

But Weedon Scott was not listening. He was thinking fast. The boat was about to leave.

"Goodbye, Matt," he said. "You don't need to write to me about the wolf. *I'll* write to *you* about him."

"I don't believe it! You're taking the wolf with you?" cried Matt.

"I certainly am!" laughed Scott.

Matt stepped off the boat onto the riverbank.

"It'll be too hot for him in the summer," he shouted.

Weedon waved goodbye from the boat. Then he turned and bent over White Fang.

"Now growl! Growl, you Wolf!" he said, as he stroked White Fang's head.

# 9

# *In Santa Clara Valley*

After a long journey by boat and train, White Fang and Weedon Scott arrived in Santa Clara Valley. This was Scott's home. When they got off the train, a man and woman were waiting for them. The woman put her arms around Scott's neck, and White Fang growled angrily. He showed his teeth. He was afraid that the woman was going to hurt his master.

"Down, Wolf!" said Scott. White Fang slowly lay down.

"Don't worry, Mother," Scott said, turning to the woman. "He was afraid that you were going to hurt me. He'll learn quickly."

A carriage—a small wooden cart pulled by horses—was waiting for them. Scott and his parents climbed into the carriage, and White Fang ran behind it.

After fifteen minutes, they turned onto a little road which led up to a large house. In front of the house was a big yard, and behind it were hills and fields. But as they came towards the house, a sheep-dog suddenly ran out towards White Fang. White Fang ran straight towards the sheep-dog, ready to bite. But as he came near, he suddenly stopped. The dog was a female. And he did not attack female dogs.

The sheep-dog did not stop, however. Sheep-dogs look after sheep. She could see that White Fang was a wolf. He was a wild animal which hurt sheep. And the sheep-dog felt fear. She jumped on White Fang and bit his shoulder. White Fang moved back. Then he tried to run past the sheep-dog. The carriage was still going towards the house, and he wanted to follow his master. But the sheep-dog kept stopping him.

"Come here, Collie!" called the man from the carriage. But Collie, the sheep-dog, was not listening. Again and again White Fang tried to run past her. But every time, she stopped him. Finally, White Fang bit Collie on the shoulder. She fell to the ground, crying angrily.

Before the sheep-dog could get up again, White Fang ran past her. He ran quickly after the carriage, which was now stopped outside the house. Collie came running after him. She was full of anger and hate for him. But Scott's father pulled her away, and Scott held White Fang back.

The carriage drove away and some more people came out of the house. Two more women put their arms around the master's neck. White Fang growled quietly, but he was not so frightened this time. Then White Fang's master took him up the steps and into the house. Inside, White Fang looked around carefully. He was waiting for something to attack him. But nothing jumped out. After a while, he lay down at his master's feet.

White Fang quickly got used to living in Santa Clara Valley. Collie, however, could not forget that wolves hurt sheep. Every time she saw White Fang, she ran at him. He walked away from her. But he would not attack her. So he stayed away from her as much as he could.

There were many other new things for White Fang in Santa Clara Valley. First, there was his master's family. Weedon's father, Judge Scott, lived in the house, with his wife and Weedon's sisters. There was also Scott's wife, Alice, and their two children. White Fang quickly learned that his master loved all these people very much. And so he knew that it was his job to watch over them carefully.

White Fang never liked the children in Gray Beaver's camp. So when his master's children first came near him, he growled. But the master taught him to be gentle with them. Soon White Fang let them stroke him and touch him. After a while he even started to like them. He never went up to them. But when they came near him he looked pleased and happy. And when they went away he looked sorry.

White Fang let everyone in the family stroke him and touch him. But he never put his head under their arms. He only did that for the master.

One night, White Fang climbed into the chicken house and killed fifty chickens. In the Wild, he killed and ate any animal he found. So he did not understand that things were different here. In the morning, his master came out and saw the dead chickens. He spoke angrily to White Fang. Then he held White Fang's nose down to the dead chickens and hit him on the head. When the master hit White Fang, it did not hurt. It was not like being hit by Gray Beaver or Beauty Smith. But he knew that the master was not pleased with him. And that hurt him more than any beating.

After that, the master took White Fang to walk among the chickens. When he saw the chickens moving around, White Fang wanted to jump at them. But as soon as he started to jump, the master stopped him. Again and again, White Fang started to jump. But every time, the master's voice stopped him. They walked among the chickens for half an hour. And after that, White Fang never killed a chicken again.

# 10

# The Blessed Wolf

There was lots of food and no work for a dog in Santa Clara Valley. So White Fang was well and happy. But he was always different from the other dogs. He followed the laws his master taught him very carefully. But there was always something fierce about him. He was still a wolf—an animal from the Wild.

White Fang never made friends with other dogs. But he learned that he did not have to attack them. He just showed them his white teeth, and growled. And they all ran away.

He learned to play-fight with his master. His master rolled him over, and White Fang pretended to be angry. But after every play-fight, the master put his arms around White Fang's neck and shoulders. Then White Fang growled his love-growl.

White Fang always went with his master when he went out on his horse. One day a rabbit suddenly ran under the horse's feet. The horse jumped, and White Fang's master fell to the ground. The fall broke his leg.

"Go home, Wolf! Go home!" the master told him.

*"Go home, Wolf! Go home!"* the master told him.

White Fang understood "home", but he did not want to leave his master. He walked away a little, and then came back, crying quietly.

"Go on, you wolf," the master said. "Go home and tell everyone. Go on!"

When White Fang arrived back at the house, the family was outside. White Fang went and stood in front of Judge Scott, growling fiercely.

"Go away, Wolf! Lie down!" said Judge Scott.

So White Fang went to the master's wife, Alice. He pulled at her dress, tearing it. Everyone was looking at him now. He stood with his head up and tried to make a noise.

"I think he's trying to speak," said the master's sister.

And at that moment, White Fang did something for the first time ever. He suddenly barked loudly.

"Something has happened to Weedon," said the master's wife at once.

They all got up, and White Fang ran down the yard. He was looking back for them to follow.

After that, everyone in the master's family had warmer feelings for White Fang. They all saw now that he was a smart wolf.

In White Fang's second year in the Santa Clara Valley, something strange happened. Collie's biting changed. Suddenly it did not hurt any more. It was playful and gentle. White Fang forgot about Collie's growling and her attacks. When she came near him now, he tried to be playful too.

One day, Collie ran in front of him down the yard and into the woods. White Fang knew that the master was going out on the horse that afternoon. The horse was waiting at the door. He stopped for a moment. But there was something in him deeper than man's law. It was deeper even than his love for the master. So when Collie bit him playfully again, he followed her. The master went out on his horse alone that day. And in the woods, White Fang ran with Collie, just like his mother and father years before.

––––––

It was at this time that a man named Jim Hall ran away from a nearby prison. Jim Hall was a terrible man. He hated everything. Then, one night, he killed three prison guards with his hands, and ran away.

All the women at Judge Scott's house were frightened. Judge Scott just laughed. But he knew Jim Hall. He sent Jim Hall to prison. And Jim Hall always said that one day he would make Judge Scott sorry for it.

White Fang, of course, knew nothing about this. But every night, the master's wife Alice waited for everyone to go to bed. Then she brought White Fang into the house. White Fang was not a house dog—he normally slept outside. So early each morning, Alice let White Fang out again.

One night, when everyone was asleep, White Fang suddenly woke up. He could hear someone in the house. A man was moving quietly towards the stairs. White Fang followed, silently. The man started moving up the stairs. Without a sound, White Fang jumped onto his back and bit his neck.

Everyone in the house woke up. There was a noise of guns. A man cried out in pain, and there was a fierce growling noise. Chairs and tables fell to the ground. Then, suddenly, everything went quiet.

Carefully, holding their guns, Weedon Scott and Judge Scott came downstairs. A man was lying dead on the floor. They looked at his face.

"Jim Hall," said Judge Scott, and the two men looked at each other.

Then they turned to White Fang. He was lying on his

side, with his eyes closed. He tried to open his eyes when the two men came close. He growled weakly when Weedon Scott stroked him. But then the growl stopped and his eyes shut once more. His body stopped moving.

"I think he's dead," said the master.

"No, he's not. Not yet," said the Judge. And he went to the telephone.

The doctor arrived very quickly. He cut White Fang open and worked on him for an hour and a half.

"He has been hurt very badly," he told the family at last. "He's lost nearly all his blood. He was shot with a gun three times. And he has many broken bones. I don't think there is much chance that he will live."

"Is there anything else we can do?" Judge Scott cried. "It doesn't matter how much it costs. We have to give him every chance he has."

"I understand that," the doctor said. "Take care of him carefully, like a sick child. And I will come back later."

Weedon's sisters, wife and mother did everything they could for White Fang. And White Fang showed the doctor that he was wrong. White Fang came from the Wild. He was used to fighting for his life. There was no weakness in him.

For weeks, he could not move. He slept a lot, and had many dreams. In his dreams, he was a cub in the cave with Kiche once more. Once again, he sat at Gray Beaver's feet, and ran away from Lip-lip. He dreamed that he was pulling Gray Beaver's sled. And he lived again his time with Beauty Smith, and the fights he fought.

Then one day, at last, the doctor took off White Fang's casts—the hard covers for his broken bones. All the family came to watch. The master rubbed White Fang's ears, and the wolf growled his love-growl. The master's wife called him "the Blessed Wolf", because he saved them all from Jim

Hall. And all the women agreed that it was a perfect name for him. White Fang tried to get up, but at first he was too weak. Again and again he tried. And at last he stood on his four legs.

"The Blessed Wolf!" cried the women.

"He'll have to learn to walk again," said the doctor. "But it won't hurt him. Take him outside now."

And White Fang walked outside, with the family all around him. He had to keep stopping to rest. But at last he arrived in the yard. There on the grass lay Collie, with six little puppies playing around her in the sun.

Collie growled warningly at White Fang, but the master pushed one puppy towards him. White Fang watched the puppy, interested, as one of the women held Collie back. Then the puppy's nose touched White Fang's nose. And White Fang put out his tongue and licked the little puppy's face.

Weedon Scott and his family cried with happiness. White Fang was surprised. He lay down and watched the puppy. Then the other puppies came climbing over him. The family cried out in excitement once again, and White Fang felt a little strange. But as the puppies went on climbing over him, he forgot about feeling strange. He lay quietly on the grass with half-shut eyes, enjoying the sun.

*He lay quietly in the grass with half-shut eyes, enjoying the sun.*

# Points for Understanding

## 1

1 Why was the she-wolf pleased when she found the small cave?
2 Why did the she-wolf growl at her mate when he came near her cubs?
3 What was special about the gray cub?

## 2

1 The gray cub found himself alone with his mother by the end of Chapter 2. What happened to:
   a) his brothers and sisters? b) his father?
2 What was the first food the gray cub found for himself?
3 What killed the mother-ptarmigan?
4 Why did the weasel not kill the gray cub?

## 3

1 What did the gray cub see by the river one morning?
2 How did the men know the she-wolf's name?
3 Why did Gray Beaver call the gray cub White Fang?
4 Why did White Fang go with the men?

## 4

1 Which two things hurt White Fang when he arrived at the camp?
2 Why could White Fang not play with the other puppies?
3 Why did Kiche not want to go back to the wild with White Fang?
4 Why did Kiche have to go away?
5 What happened when White Fang tried to follow her?

# 5

1 What two important things did White Fang learn about fighting?
2 Why did the men and dogs hate White Fang?
3 What was the agreement between dog and man?
4 Who was White Fang pleased to see in the camp one day?
5 Why did she not remember him?
6 Why did White Fang run away to the forest?
7 Which dog did he kill while he was living in the forest?

# 6

1 Why did Gray Beaver go to Fort Yukon?
2 What did White Fang do at Fort Yukon?
3 Why did Beauty Smith go to see Gray Beaver?
4 Why did Gray Beaver sell White Fang in the end?
5 White Fang ran away from Beauty Smith twice. How did he get free?

# 7

1 Why did men come to watch White Fang?
2 What did White Fang do for the first time when he fought with the bull-dog?
3 How did the bull-dog win the fight with White Fang?
4 Why did Scott put a gun in the bull-dog's mouth?
5 How much money did Scott pay Beauty Smith for White Fang?

# 8

1 What happened when Major ate White Fang's meat?
2 Why did Scott and Matt decide not to kill White Fang?
3 Why did White Fang become sick?
4 Scott and Matt were surprised to see White Fang on the boat. How did White Fang get out of the cabin?
5 What did Weedon Scott decide to do with White Fang?

## 9

1 Why did White Fang not attack Collie, the sheep-dog?
2 What did White Fang kill at the Scotts' home?
3 How did Weedon Scott stop this happening again?

## 10

1 How did White Fang help his master when he fell off his horse?
2 Who became White Fang's mate?
3 Why did Alice let White Fang sleep in the house at night?
4 How did White Fang attack Jim Hall?
5 What did the women call White Fang after he saved them from Jim Hall?

# Exercises

## Vocabulary: meanings of words from the story

**Put the words and phrases in the box next to the correct meanings.**

Yukon   guard   frozen   expert   cub   sniff   cave   lair   roll   weasel
fierce   tepee   woods   sled   lick   famine   hunger   throat   master
hawk   gold rush   fence   growl   bark   chain   stick   confused
danger   mine   cabin   rub   stroke   cage   hunt   marks   mate

| | | |
|---|---|---|
| 1 | | an animal's sexual partner |
| 2 | | to find and kill animals for food or for their skin |
| 3 | | very cold – turned to ice |
| 4 | | a bad situation in which you can be hurt or killed |
| 5 | | a young wolf (bear, lion, fox) |
| 6 | | to move your tongue over something to eat it, clean it, or make it wet |
| 7 | | a large hole in the side of a hill or under the ground |
| 8 | | the feeling you have when there is nothing to eat |
| 9 | | a place where a wild animal lives – especially a wolf |
| 10 | | to move forward and turn over and over |
| 11 | | a large bird that kills animals for food |
| 12 | | a small, thin animal with brown fur, short legs and a long tail – and sharp teeth |
| 13 | | strong anger or hate and ready to attack with force |
| 14 | | a large area of Canada which is next to Alaska |
| 15 | | a tall, round tent made of animal skins – a North American Indian word |

63

| 16 | | a place where many trees grow (smaller than a forest) |
|----|---|---|
| 17 | | a vehicle for travelling over snow – it does not have wheels, it has skis |
| 18 | | a serious lack of food that makes people die |
| 19 | | the front part of your neck (also the area at the back of your mouth) |
| 20 | | a time when a lot of people went to a place to look for gold, hoping to become rich (California 1848, Yukon / Klondike 1897) |
| 21 | | a frightening or unfriendly low noise made by a dog or wolf |
| 22 | | the loud short sound made by a dog |
| 23 | | a series of metal rings joined to each other – it is used for fastening things |
| 24 | | a thin piece of wood that has been cut or broken from a tree (this word has more than one meaning) |
| 25 | | someone who has a particular skill or knows a lot about a subject – usually an important person |
| 26 | | a large hole or tunnel where people take coal or metal out of the ground (this word has more than one meaning) |
| 27 | | a small, simple wooden house in the mountains or in a forest |
| 28 | | a person who has control over other people (especially servants and slaves) and animals |
| 29 | | to press and move your hands over a surface |
| 30 | | a gentle movement of your hand over skin or hair or fur (this word has more than one meaning) |
| 31 | | not able to understand something or think clearly about it |
| 32 | | an upright structure made of wood or wire that surrounds an area of land |

| 33 | | a container made of wire or metal bars – used for keeping birds and animals |
| 34 | | areas of colour on something – such as an animal's skin – that is different in colour from the rest (this word has many meanings) |
| 35 | | to smell something in order to learn about it |
| 36 | | to protect; also a person or animal who protects someone |

## Writing: rewrite sentences

**Rewrite sentences using the words and phrases in the box to replace the underlined words. You may need to change tenses. There are two extra words.**

**Example:** *The time of year when things begin to grow was coming.*
You write: *Spring was coming.*

~~Spring~~ frozen very dangerous entrance hunting lair camp pack die live fangs tepees growl puppies hurt hunger whiskey master expert bark shut agreement coat

1 The <u>place where you went in</u> to the cave was small.

The _____

2 It was a few miles up a small <u>icy</u> river.

It was _____

3 The gray cub found out about <u>what it was like to have no food</u>.

The gray _____

4 The she-wolf left her cubs and went out <u>looking for food.</u>

The she-wolf _____

5 She went past the lynx's <u>resting place</u>.

She went _____

6  A group of wolves could frighten a lynx.

A
_____

7  For a lone wolf, lynxes were a big threat.

For a lone
_____

8  The gray wolf's brothers and sisters did not live long.

The gray wolf's
_____

9  His nose was painful.

His nose
_____

10  It looks like a dog, but it has the teeth of a wolf.

It looks like
_____

11  The Indians lived in tents made from animal skin.

The Indians
_____

12  The biggest of the young dogs was called Lip-Lip.

The biggest
_____

13  Most dogs made a low noise in their throats before they attacked.

Most dogs
_____

14  White Fang learned that there was an understanding between dog
    and man.

White Fang learned
_____

15  Beauty Smith gave strong alcoholic drink to Gray Beaver.

Beauty Smith
_____

16  White Fang had a new owner – Beauty Smith.

White Fang had
_____

17  Weedon Scott is a mining professional.

Weedon Scott is
_____

18  For the first time, White Fang made the noise of a dog.

For the first
_____

19  I don't think there is much chance that he will survive.

I don't think
_____

20  He lay in the sun and his eyes were half <u>closed</u>.

He lay in

## Grammar: a little / little; a few / few; less; slightly

**Choose the correct word in the following sentences.**

> **Example:**   *The color of her coat was ~~little~~ / slightly red.*

1  There was little / slightly food to eat in winter.

2  The wolves saw a little / few men in the woods.

3  Every year there was fewer / less food in the mountains.

4  Only a little / a few of the animals survived until summer.

5  Cherokee moved his mouth little / slightly closer to White Fang's throat.

## Grammar: verb / verb *-ing*

**Choose the correct verb form in the following sentences.**

> **Example:**   *The snow was deep and ~~to walk~~ / walking was difficult.*

1  He had to fight / fighting the pack of dogs.

2  White Fang learned to attack / attacking as fast as possible.

3  He knocked the dog over and killed / killing it.

4  The Indians went hunt / hunting food every day.

5  White Fang became strong after eat / eating meat.

6  Gray Beaver made money by sell / selling furs to the gold hunters.

7  Many gold hunters came / coming to the Yukon in 1898.

8  Beauty Smith started bring / bringing whiskey to the camp.

9  He enjoyed have / having power over men and animals weaker than himself.

10  Gray Beaver went home while White Fang stayed / staying with Beauty Smith.

11  White Fang never stopped growl / growling at Beauty Smith.

12  "I'm not sell / selling the dog," said Beauty Smith.

## Grammar: correct the mistakes

**Rewrite the following sentences, correcting the mistakes.**

> **Example:**  *Above the trees were a mountain.*
> You write:  *Above the trees was a mountain.*

1  The cub growled fierce at the world.



2  He felt teeth bit into his body.



3  Lip-lip did not seem danger.



4  Gray Beaver never stroke White Fang's back.



5  White Fang was starting like camp life.



6  At last his money was all went.



7  He hated this terrible manimal, Beauty Smith.



8  Matt stepped off the boat into the riverbank.



9  It doesn't matter how much does it cost.



10  He was used to fight for his life.

# Vocabulary and grammar: anagrams

One word is missing from each sentence. The letters of the missing words are mixed up. Write the words correctly and complete the sentences.

| Example: SHINNEUS | Her mate went out alone into the bright _____. |
| You write: | Her mate went out alone into the bright sunshine. |

| 1 | STERMA | White Fang followed his _____ everywhere. |
|---|--------|----------------------------------------------|
| 2 | ECRIFE | He was already a _____ little cub. |
| 3 | THINGIT | Gray Beaver stopped _____ him. |
| 4 | CLETAXY | He learned to do _____ what Gray Beaver told him. |
| 5 | GRINWAN | White Fang learned to attack without any _____. |
| 6 | RUGHNY | One day he met a pack of _____ wolves. |
| 7 | DAININ | The _____ dogs jumped on the white men's dogs. |
| 8 | CHALICOOL | He started bringing whiskey — a strong _____ drink. |
| 9 | GENTSORTS | He was the _____ dog in the pack. |
| 10 | BLETRIER | That year, a _____ thing happened. |

## Grammar: syntax

**Put the words into the correct order to make sentences.**

> **Example:** *Matt stepped onto the boat out of the riverbank.*
> You write: *Matt stepped out of the boat onto the riverbank.*

1 an animal could kill You by biting its throat.

_____

2 his mother to come He wanted with him.

_____

3 The ground hardly touched the bull-dog's feet.

_____

4 Beauty Smith fights for the chain let him only ever off.

_____

5 White Fang gave His voice a strange, safe feeling.

_____

6 The man ate White Fang and threw them some more bits of meat.

_____

7 Scott He saw into a big bag packing things.

_____

8 a little White Fang was Sitting way away.

_____

# Vocabulary choice: words which are related in meaning

Which word is most closely related? Look at the example then circle the word which is most closely related to the word in bold.

| Example: | | | | |
|---|---|---|---|---|
| **mate** | captain | (partner) | cook | seaman |

| | | | | | |
|---|---|---|---|---|---|
| 1 | **hunt** | search | find | eat | food |
| 2 | **cub** | taxi | hat | puppy | scout |
| 3 | **lick** | like | smoke | toast | tongue |
| 4 | **lair** | shelter | fur | shoes | trader |
| 5 | **lock** | fasten | see | lake | hair |
| 6 | **fang** | football | wind | bird | tooth |
| 7 | **fierce** | afraid | angry | sharp | blood |
| 8 | **throat** | hand | leg | arm | neck |
| 9 | **pack** | lunch | group | biscuit | behind |
| 10 | **stroke** | rub | fire | bat | stick |
| 11 | **cabin** | brick | firewood | hut | camp |
| 12 | **bark** | canoe | plant | wolf | noise |
| 13 | **beat** | hit | drum | light | quiet |

# Vocabulary: opposite meanings

Which word is nearest to the opposite meaning?

| Example: | | | | |
|---|---|---|---|---|
| **dangerous** | risky | wild | animal | (safe) |

| | | | | | |
|---|---|---|---|---|---|
| 1 | **famine** | starvation | hunger | plenty | thirst |
| 2 | **terrible** | wonderful | dreadful | poor | fearful |
| 3 | **strong** | week | tough | hard | weak |
| 4 | **exciting** | fun | thrilling | boring | interesting |
| 5 | **moving** | mobile | quick | traveling | still |
| 6 | **perfect** | right | wrong | good | just |
| 7 | **show** | explain | hide | tell | picture |
| 8 | **master** | owner | boss | servant | skilled |

Published by Macmillan Heinemann ELT
Between Towns Road, Oxford OX4 3PP
A division of Macmillan Publishers Limited
Companies and representatives throughout the world
Heinemann is the registered trademark of Pearson Education, used under licence.

ISBN 978–0–230–03440–2
ISBN 978–0–230–02673–5 (with CD pack)

This version of *White Fang* by Jack London was retold by
Rachel Bladon for Macmillan Readers

First published 2008
Text © Macmillan Publishers Limited 2008
Design and illustration © Macmillan Publishers Limited 2008
This version first published 2008

Illustrated by John Dillow and Martin Sanders
Cover photo by Corbis/Zefa

Printed and bound in Thailand

2013 2012 2011
8  7  6  5  4

with CD pack
2013 2012 2011
9  8  7  6  5